MY FAVORITE DOG

GREYHOUNDS

by Colton Temple

Kaleidoscope
Minneapolis, MN

The Quest for Discovery Never Ends

This edition first published in 2022 by Kaleidoscope Publishing, Inc.

For information regarding permission, write to
Kaleidoscope Publishing, Inc.
6012 Blue Circle Drive
Minnetonka, MN 55343

Library of Congress Control Number
2021934865

ISBN
978-1-64519-466-8 (library bound)
978-1-64519-474-3 (ebook)

Printed in the United States of America.

FIND ME
IF YOU CAN!

Bigfoot lurks within one of the images in this book. It's up to you to find him!

TABLE OF CONTENTS

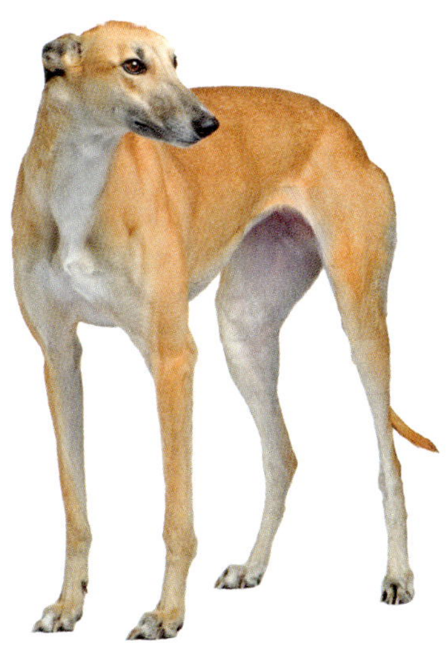

Introduction

A Race to the Finish!

Carlos grips the track fence. The race is about to begin. He tries to catch a glimpse of Rocket, but Rocket and the other Greyhounds are already in the starting box. Greyhound racing is illegal in most states. When a dog starts losing, it is often abandoned or put down. Carlos wants to rescue Rocket.

The starting box opens. The Greyhounds launch forward as they chase the **lure**. Carlos spots Rocket. He's in the middle of the pack. The dogs round the final stretch. They near the finish line. Rocket falls behind! He comes in last! Carlos looks for his dad. He's shaking hands with Rocket's owner. Carlos shouts with joy. Rocket can **retire**! Carlos gets to bring him home!

FUN FACT

Greyhounds are the fastest dogs. They can run up to 45 miles (72 kilometers) per hour!

Chapter 1

The Story of Greyhounds

Five thousand years ago, Greyhounds were the dogs of pharaohs! Only royalty and nobles could own them. Egyptian rulers bred Greyhounds to sprint across the desert to detect, chase, and capture quick desert animals for sport and food. Egyptians believed their pharaohs were gods chosen to rule them on Earth. They also believed their rulers' beautiful Greyhounds were an example of their **divine** power. Egyptians treasured Greyhounds so much that they often showed them in **hieroglyphics**. They also **mummified** and buried Greyhounds with their pharaohs.

Egyptian hieroglyphics

NOBLE DOGS FOR NOBLE PEOPLE

These noble-looking dogs were the pets of many great leaders and royalty throughout history. Cleopatra, Christopher Columbus, Teddy Roosevelt, General George Custer, Babe Ruth, Betty White, Queen Victoria, and King Henry VIII all owned Greyhounds.

A Basset Hound

A Dachshund

A Beagle

Greyhounds still look noble. But now, like other hounds, they can be owned by anyone. Dog breeds are put into groups. Greyhounds are in the Hound Group. Dogs in the Hound Group have many different histories, but they were all bred to hunt. A few other dogs in the Hound Group are Basset Hounds, Beagles, and Dachshunds.

Even before Egyptian hieroglyphics, Greyhounds were shown chasing game in prehistoric art.

Carlos and his dad arrive home with Rocket after taking him to the **veterinarian**. Before opening the car door, Carlos puts a leash on him. Greyhounds like Rocket were bred to hunt using sight. Instead of sniffing out prey, they use their keen eyesight to spot game. Carlos doesn't want Rocket to run off if he sees a squirrel or other small animal. Leash secured, Carlos opens the door, and Rocket jumps out.

"Welcome to your new home, Rocket!" Carlos says.

Once inside, Rocket wags his tail and weaves through the furniture to the soft dog bed by the couch. He snuggles into the toys Carlos bought him. Carlos thinks he already looks right at home. The vet told him Greyhounds have a lot of energy and need to exercise, but they are also happy relaxing and lounging around the house all day. Carlos sits down next to Rocket. Rocket rolls over so Carlos can scratch his belly. *No wonder Egyptians loved these dogs,* Carlos thinks as he pets Rocket.

Where
GREYHOUNDS
come from
Mediterranean Sea
ASIA
EGYPT
AFRICA
Red Sea
COUNTRY OF ORIGIN
N
W
E
S

Chapter 2

Looking at a Greyhound

Carlos holds the leash up. "Want to go to the dog park, Rocket?" Rocket sits up and wags his long tail. Carlos pats his short coat. Greyhounds can be many colors, including brindle, black, white, red, blue, which is a gray color, or fawn, which is a light yellow-brown color. They can also be any combination of these colors.

A brindle Greyhound

A fawn Greyhound

A black Greyhound

SPOT THE SIGHTHOUND

There are many similar breeds to Greyhounds. And they all hunt by sight. Keep an eye out for these super seers:

SPANISH GALGO
Height:* 23-27 inches (58-69 cm)

SALUKI
Height:* 23-28 inches (58-71 cm)

BORZOI
Height:* 26-28 inches (66-71 cm)

ITALIAN GREYHOUND
Height:* 13-15 inches (33-38 cm)

*Height at shoulder

SIZE COMPARISON

GREYHOUND, GALGO, SALUKI, BORZOI

ITALIAN GREYHOUND

THE GREYHOUND

MALES

HEIGHT:*
28-30 inches (71-76 cm)

WEIGHT:
65-70 pounds
(29-32 kg)

FEMALES

HEIGHT:*
27-28 inches (69-71 cm)

WEIGHT:
60-65 pounds (27-29 kg)

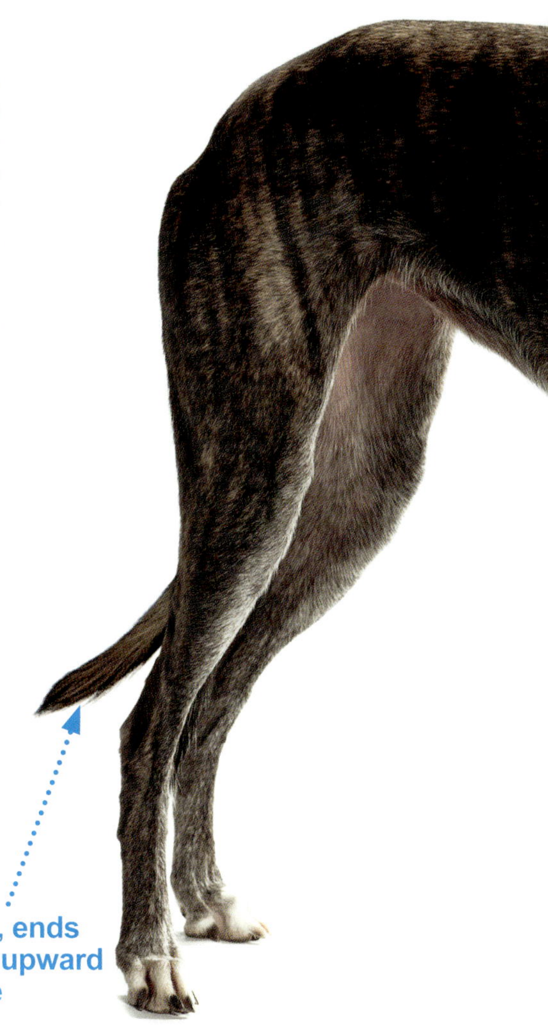

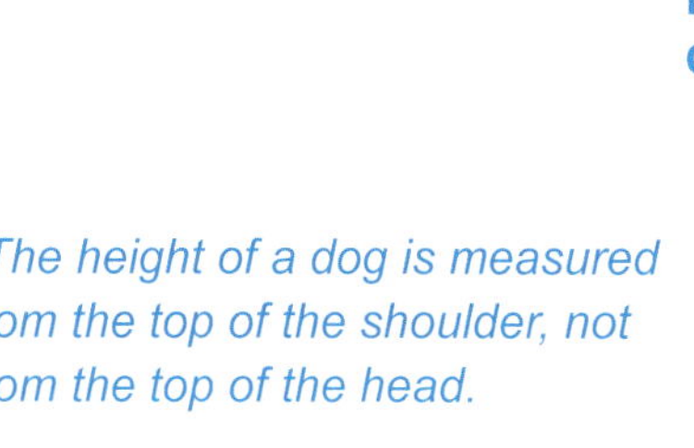

**The height of a dog is measured from the top of the shoulder, not from the top of the head.*

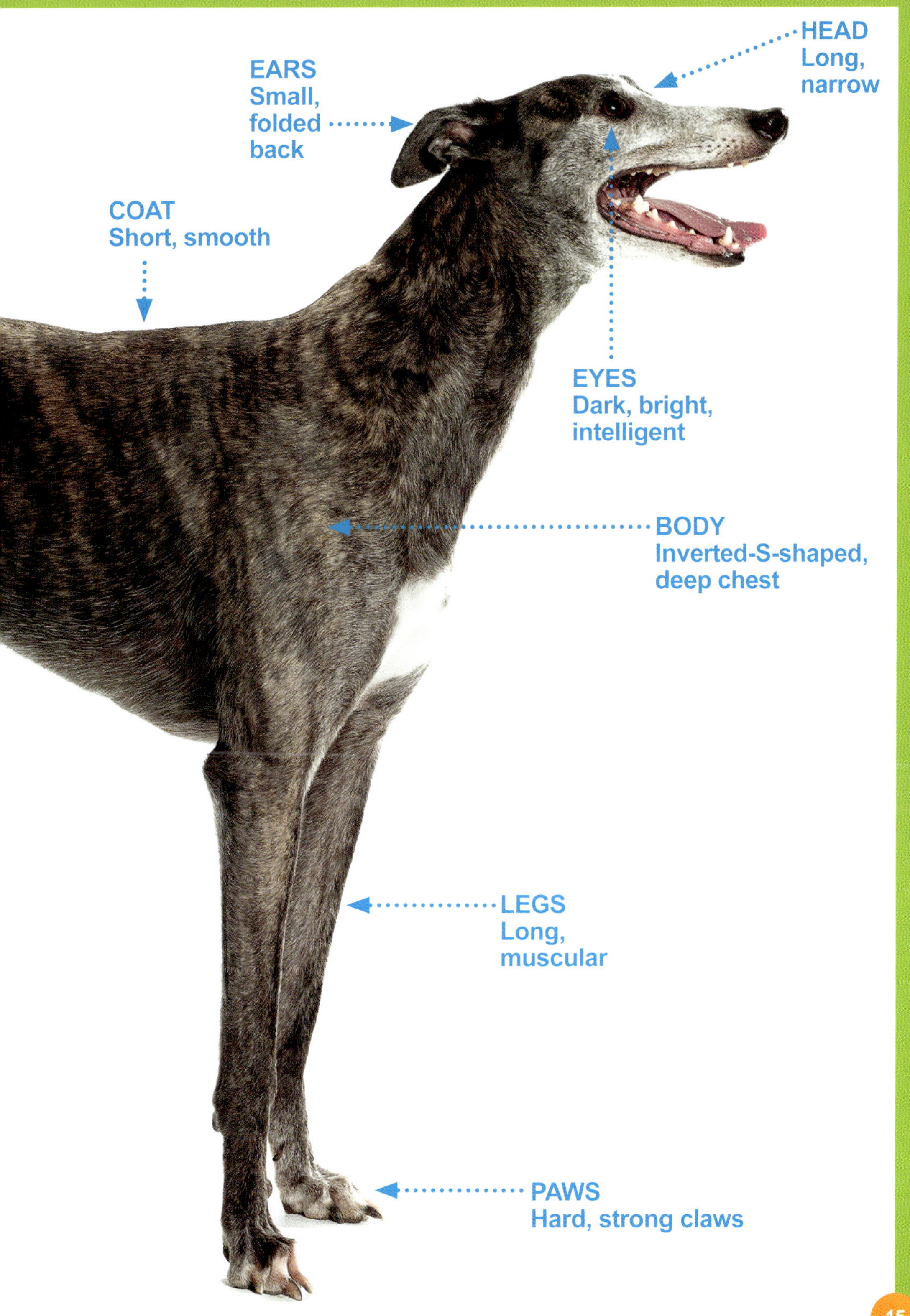
HEAD
Long,
narrow
EARS
Small,
folded
back
COAT
Short, smooth
EYES
Dark, bright,
intelligent
BODY
Inverted-S-shaped,
deep chest
LEGS
Long,
muscular
PAWS
Hard, strong claws

FUN FACT
When running, Greyhounds spend 75% of their time in the air!

Carlos and Rocket enter the dog park. "Stay close," Carlos says as he takes off Rocket's leash. Even if Rocket sees prey, the park is fenced in, so he can't go far. Rocket leaves to play with other dogs. Carlos smiles at how easily and fast Rocket runs. He looks like he's flying!

BRED FOR SPEED!

Everything about Greyhounds' bodies makes them fast. Their narrow heads cut through the air easily. Their paws are like springs. And their strong muscles and long legs make their strides long. It only takes six strides for Greyhounds to reach full speed!

Chapter 3

Meet a Greyhound!

Carlos doesn't know how Rocket will act around the other dogs. He's only ever seen Rocket race them. Rocket spots a German Shorthaired Pointer and trots up to him. Before Carlos can call him back, the two are playing like puppies. "Good boy, Rocket!" Carlos praises.

QUICK LEARNERS

Greyhound puppies are smart. They learn quickly. But keep the lessons short, or they'll become bored. Dogs learn better with kind words rather than harsh words. If they do something you don't like, ignore them. Show them a lot of new things and give them praise and treats. This way, they'll know the new things are safe. Otherwise, they might chase every animal they see.

After an hour, the German Shorthaired Pointer's owner calls him away. Rocket quickly returns to Carlos. He leans against his leg as he stares after his new friend. "Don't worry, Rocket." Carlos pats his head. "I bet you'll see each other again." Though Greyhounds are affectionate with their family members, they are usually timid around strangers and may stick close to their owners when they feel shy.

Another dog wants to play, but Rocket looks sleepy. Greyhounds don't need to play for hours or go on long jogs. They only need time and space to sprint around for a bit. Carlos clips on Rocket's leash. "Ready to go home?" Carlos asks. Rocket readily heads for the dog park gate. Carlos loves how quickly Rocket has warmed up to him. He's so happy he can give Rocket a good home.

FUN FACT

Greyhounds are usually calm. They are often considered one of the gentlest dog breeds.

Chapter 4

Caring for a Greyhound

Like other Greyhounds, Rocket doesn't need a lot of grooming, but Carlos gets the tub ready. Rocket is muddy after playing in the park! Carlos suds up Rocket's short coat. He uses a dog shampoo recommended by the vet.

The vet also told Carlos to check Rocket's ears for **debris** or wax. If there's a lot, he could get an **infection**. Rocket shakes himself dry before Carlos can cover him with the towel. It looks like Carlos took a bath, too!

Besides baths, Greyhounds can also be cleaned with a damp cloth or hound glove. This is a hairbrush that is like a glove.

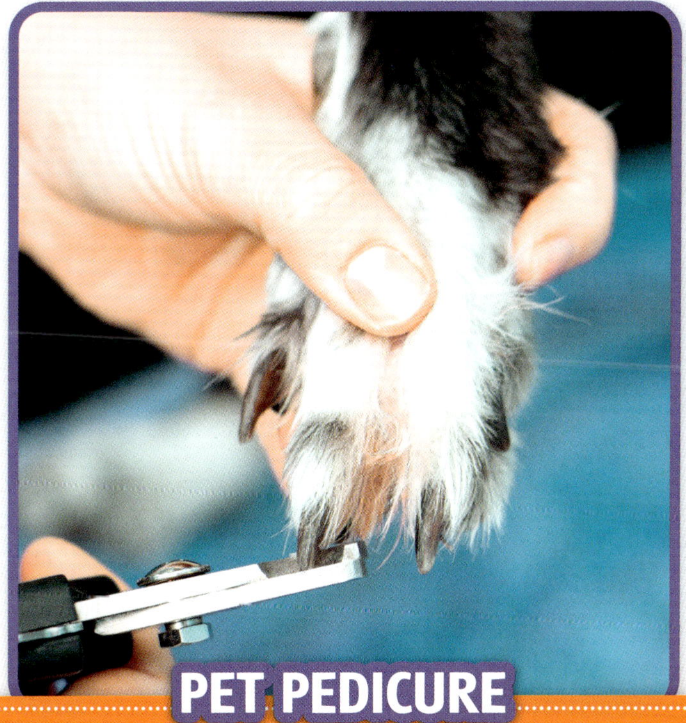

PET PEDICURE

Greyhounds have fast-growing nails. They can wear down if they run enough, but if not, the nails will get long. Carlos knows to trim Rocket's nails regularly. Long nails can be uncomfortable for Greyhounds.

Carlos scoops dog food into Rocket's bowl. He makes sure he has fresh water. "Dinnertime, Rocket!" Rocket strolls in and eagerly eats his food. Greyhounds burn a lot of energy when they run. The vet told Carlos to give him dog food with higher **calories** and **protein**.

FUN FACT

Protein is key to having energy. It fuels the body and helps repair muscles after exercise so they can grow stronger.

Make sure to keep your dog happy and healthy by providing it with daily fresh water and a clean water bowl.

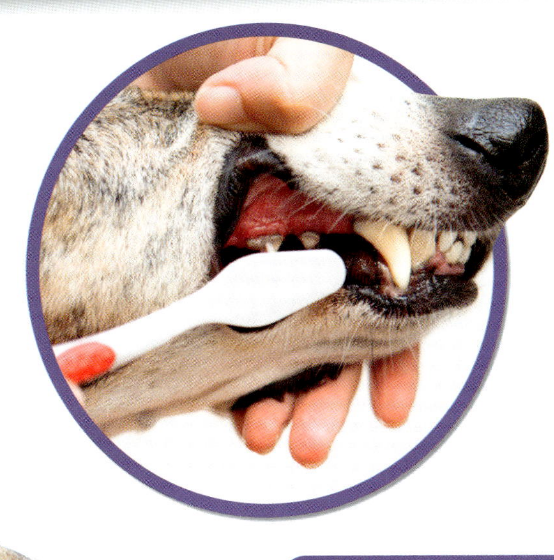

Never use human toothpaste to clean your dog's teeth. It will make it sick.

Dogs need their teeth cleaned just like humans. Rocket must like the taste of his dog toothpaste because he tries to lick it off the brush before Carlos can get to his teeth. Carlos laughs, "We'll try again tomorrow."

"Want to sleep on the bed?" Carlos asks and pats the covers. Rocket jumps up. "Good boy, Rocket." Carlos pulls back the blanket to get in. All of Rocket's toys are in the bed. Greyhounds sometimes like to collect toys and shoes. "I guess this is your room now, too." Carlos pets Rocket's head as they both fall asleep. He's glad his family rescued a Greyhound. Rocket already feels like family.

FUN FACT
Some Greyhounds sleep with their eyes open.

After reading the book, it's time to think about what you learned. Try the following exercises to jump-start your ideas.

THINK

FIND OUT MORE. There is so much more to dig up about Greyhounds. What do you want to learn? Find out more on the American Kennel Club website. Or look for a Greyhound club in your area. You can meet people who love them as much as you do!

CREATE

ART TIME. Can you draw a Greyhound? Look up a cute picture and grab some markers and paper. Will your pup have a fancy hairstyle? Will it wear a fun hat? What is its favorite toy or game? Does it have a job? The sky is the limit!

SHARE

THE MORE WHO KNOW. Share what you learned about Greyhounds. Use your own words to write a paragraph. What are the main ideas of this book? What facts from the book can you use to support those ideas? Share your paragraph with a classmate. Do they have any comments or questions about Greyhounds?

GROW

HELP OUT! There are dogs near you that need care. Animal shelters can be great places to volunteer and hang out with pups. Contact a shelter near you and find out if you can help. Or can your family donate food or gear to help rescue dogs? Find out why dogs end up in shelters. Is there anything you can do to help them find homes?

RESEARCH NINJA

Visit www.ninjaresearcher.com/4668 to learn how to take your research skills and book report writing to the next level!

Research

SEARCH LIKE A PRO

Learn how to use search engines to find useful websites.

FACT OR FAKE

Discover how you can tell a trusted website from an untrustworthy resource.

TEXT DETECTIVE

Explore how to zero in on the information you need most.

SHOW YOUR WORK

Research responsibly–learn how to cite sources.

Write

GET TO THE POINT

Learn how to express your main ideas.

PLAN OF ATTACK

Learn prewriting exercises and create an outline.

Further Resources

BOOKS

Blake, Kevin. *Dog Heroes: Rescue Dogs*. Minneapolis, Minn.: Bearport Publishing, 2016.

Bozzo, Linda. *Discover Dogs with the American Canine Association: I like Greyhounds!* New York, N.Y.: Enslow Publishing, 2017.

Shaffer, Lindsay. *Awesome Dogs: Greyhounds*. Minnetonka, Minn.: Bellwether Media, Inc., 2019.

WEBSITES

FACTSURFER

Factsurfer.com gives you a safe, fun way to find more information.

1. Go to www.factsurfer.com.
2. Enter "Greyhounds" into the search box and click 🔍
3. Select your book cover to see a list of related websites.

Glossary

calories: a unit of energy. The more calories a food or drink has, the more energy it could give you. If you don't exercise and use the calories though, a lot of calories can be unhealthy.

debris: little pieces of waste, usually after something breaks.

divine: something from or like a god.

hieroglyphics: an Egyptian writing form that used pictures instead of words.

infection: when something enters the body and makes it sick.

lure: a mechanical device that races around the track. It has bait on it so Greyhounds will chase it.

mummified: an ancient way of preserving a body. Egyptians prepared the body and wrapped it in cloth before burying it. This helped the bodies last longer.

protein: an important food group. Protein helps repair and build up the body. It also gives you energy. People often eat meat and eggs for protein.

retire: to leave a job or sport at the end of a career. Animals that race retire when they can't race or are too slow.

stride: how an animal or person walks.

veterinarian: a doctor for animals.

Index

PHOTO CREDITS

The images in this book are reproduced through the courtesy of: TrapezaStudio/Shutterstock Images, cover, p. 1; Maximillian Laschon/Shutterstock Images, p. 1 (paw prints); p. 3; EcoPrint/Shutterstock Images, p. 4-5 (top); Hedser van Brug/Shutterstock Images, p. 4-5 (bottom); Sompol/Shutterstock Images, p. 6; Rosa Frei/Shutterstock Images, p. 7 (top); Everett Collection/Shutterstock Images, p. 7 (bottom); Susan Schmitz/Shutterstock Images, p. 8 (top); BIGANDT.COM/Shutterstock Images, p. 8 (middle); Svetography/Shutterstock Images, p. 8 (bottom left); Dmitry Pichugin/Shutterstock Images, p. 8 (bottom right); MVolodymyr/Shutterstock Images, p. 9; Rhys Leonard/Shutterstock Images, p. 10; Joy Baldassarre/Shutterstock Images, p. 12 (top); Eric Isselee/Shutterstock Images, p. 12 (bottom left); Gelpi/Shutterstock Images, p. 12 (bottom right); Eric Isselee/Shutterstock Images, p. 13 (top right); orangephoto/Shutterstock Images, p. 13 (top left); Jagodka/Shutterstock Images, p. 13 (middle right); TrapezaStudio/Shutterstock Images, p. 13 (bottom left); Dan Kosmayer/Shutterstock Images, p. 14-15; Bildagentur Zoonar GmbH/Shutterstock Images, p. 16-17; Utekhina Anna/Shutterstock Images, p. 18; Rita_Kochmarjova/Shutterstock Images, p. 19; Capuski/iStockphoto, p. 20 (top); Susan Schmitz/Shutterstock Images, p. 20-21 (bottom); everydoghasastory/Shutterstock Images, p. 21 (top); Sergio Arjona/Shutterstock Images, p. 22 (top); Dalaifood/Shutterstock Images, p. 22 (bottom); GaiBru Photo/Shutterstock Images, p. 23; Fotievna/Shutterstock Images, p. 24 (left); TierneyMJ/Shutterstock Images, p. 25 (left); Celiafoto/Shutterstock Images, p. 25; Dalaifood/Shutterstock Images, p. 25 (right); everydoghasastory/Shutterstock Images, p. 26-27; Eric Isselee/Shutterstock Images, p. 30.

About the Author

Colton Temple is a published writer who enjoys the outdoors. He has written many children's books about animals from all around the world. He believes the best way to write about animals is to visit where they live. He's even been scuba diving in the ocean! Temple lives in Minnesota with his energetic puppy, Jack.